ALSO BY PAMELA PRINCE

*Best of Friends*
CLASSIC ILLUSTRATIONS OF CHILDREN AND ANIMALS

*Toyland*
CLASSIC ILLUSTRATIONS OF CHILDREN AND THEIR TOYS

*Once Upon a Time*
INSPIRED BY THE ART OF JESSIE WILLCOX SMITH

*Sweet Dreams*
THE ART OF BESSIE PEASE GUTMANN

# A Day with Josephine and Her Friends

by Pamela Prince • Inspired by the artwork of Honor C. Appleton

Based on the books by Mrs. H. C. Cradock

Harmony Books • New York

Published by Harmony Books, a division of Crown Publishers, Inc., 201 East 50th Street, New York, New York 10022. Member of the Crown Publishing Group.

HARMONY and colophon are trademarks of Crown Publishers, Inc.

Manufactured in Japan

Design by Heidi North

Library of Congress Cataloging-in-Publication Data
Prince, Pamela.
A day with Josephine and her friends/by Pamela Prince:
inspired by the artwork of Honor C. Appleton; based on the books by
Mrs. H. C. Cradock.
1. Appleton, Honor C.—Themes, motives. I. Appleton, Honor C.
II. Cradock, H. C., Mrs. III. Title.
NC978.5.A67P75 1992
741.6'42—dc20 91-21934
CIP
AC

ISBN 0-517-58303-8

10 9 8 7 6 5 4 3 2 1

First Edition

*For my mother*

I *was delightfully surprised* when I recently discovered some old and dusty volumes of the Josephine book series, filled with Honor C. Appleton's delightful watercolor pen-and-ink illustrations, in a London antiquarian stall. Having collected illustrated children's books for many years, I wondered how her work could have escaped unnoticed. When I returned to the United States, I was further amazed that the books were unknown to rare book dealers who have specialized in this field far longer than I have. Therefore, it is with pleasure that I introduce this book, with hopes that a new audience and a new generation might become familiar with this English illustrator's talent and with the charming characters her artwork brought to life.

The Josephine series, created in partnership by Appleton and the writer Mrs. H. C. Cradock, was published in Great Britain by Blackie and Son Limited, from 1916 through the 1930s, and enjoyed much popular appeal. A 1990 retrospective show of Appleton's original artwork at the Chris Beetles Limited, Gallery in London attracted many people who fondly recalled the Josephine books as treasured memories from their childhoods. But the books were not reprinted and the text seemed somewhat dated and overly sentimental. The illustrations, though, retain a remarkable delicacy and freshness. Josephine continues to radiate sweetness and energy, while her entourage of toys and dolls, led by the frisky Quacky

Jack, appear bright-eyed and filled with fun. To showcase Appleton's artwork, I have respectfully created a new text that allows today's reader to appreciate this nostalgic imagery in a new way.

Honor Charlotte Appleton was born on February 4, 1879, in Brighton, and, encouraged by her mother, Georgina, was executing skillful watercolors by the time she was ten years old. She studied at the Royal Academy of Art and published her first illustrated book by 1902. In 1910 she illustrated William Blake's poems *Songs of Innocence,* and, over the next forty years, went on to illustrate over 150 children's books. Like her American contemporary, the artist Jessie Wilcox Smith, Appleton's prolific body of work and her productivity appear to have left little time for any flamboyant personal life. What little is known of Honor C. Appleton appears to speak for a modest, organized life devoted to art and career. She died on December 30, 1951, tended by her sister Sissy, in Sussex.

Her work leaves us with a personal vision of childhood. She created innocence without sentimentality, mischief without harm, beauty with a deft and delicate touch. I hope you enjoy this introduction to her work and find a day spent with Josephine and her friends to be a pleasurable time.

*Pamela Prince*

Teddy, who had already been up for some time, greeted Josephine. "Good morning. Hurry, now! John will be here soon and he'll want to play."

When she finished dressing, Josephine brushed Morgan, the puppy, and, after a little breakfast, they were all ready.

As soon as John arrived,
the children went straight to the toy
closet. Josephine threw open the doors and
bright morning light streamed in upon all the dolls and
toys. They blinked their eyes at such a sudden awakening,
and when Josephine called out, "Time to get up! Time for
school!" a bit of grumbling could be heard.

Quacky Jack, up on the shelf, squawked, "Can't we sleep a
little longer?"

"No, you can't," replied Josephine. Quacky was her favorite
but he always tried to get his own way. She wanted to start
things off properly this morning. "We'll have our lessons
first," she announced, "and then we can play
all day!"

At that, everyone hopped up and
scrambled down.

The first toy to arrive at the schoolroom was Quacky Jack, of course. The door squeaked open and he said, "Yoo-hoo! I'm here!"

"Since you're the first, you may begin by reciting your ABC's," said Josephine in a serious voice.

Quacky Jack saw this as a chance to show off, but he never could remember if P came before Q or the other way around, and when he got to L, M, N, O, he mixed it up by saying M, N, L, O.

He did spell DUCK just perfectly though.

When it was Angelina's turn she said the alphabet frontwards and backwards, counted to one hundred with her eyes closed, and spelled out the word "chrysanthemum." The other dolls were extremely impressed, especially the two Japanese dolls, Suki and Yoshiko.

So was Josephine. So much so that she called, "School is dismissed for the day!"

Everyone skipped their way right back to the playroom, where John had promised to tell them a story.

While John told the tale, the toys listened quietly.

Morgan, the mischievous puppy, never could sit still for story-time, and this morning he decided to have a mid-morning snack instead. Only Quacky noticed that the troublemaking young fellow had chosen a lace curtain to nibble on.

The children didn't notice. They left the room to get a bite to eat for themselves, and while they were away Morgan continued to misbehave. Why, he tried to eat the dolls!

"Help! Oh, help!" shrieked the others. Yoshiko ran to fetch Josephine and Quacky stamped his feet.

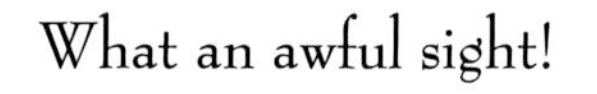

What an awful sight!

"Who could have done such a nasty thing?" Josephine wondered, as she and John surveyed the terrible pile of injured dolls.

Quacky Jack was in the middle of the floor, a bit squashed. "Call a doctor," he pleaded.

The playroom became a hospital and soon everyone had their arms screwed back in and their heads faced in the right direction. Nurse Josephine bandaged Clementine and cradled her in her arms, before placing the doll into a cozy shoebox for a rest.

Dora and Quacky, only slightly injured, made a speedy recovery. "It was Morgan!" they shouted. "It was Morgan, the puppy, who attacked us!"

"Justice will be served," promised Josephine and John. "We'll track down that criminal wherever he may be."

They found the puppy underneath the babydoll's table, sleeping peacefully and softly snoring. "He looks quite innocent," thought Josephine. "Could he really be the one responsible for all the mischief?"

Morgan was brought back into the playroom for his trial, where every doll accused him. There was no denying what he had done.

John and Josephine gave him a solemn lecture. "You mustn't, ever again, treat the dolls and toys in that rough manner," said Josephine. "We treat you gently and kindly, and you must act in the same way. Now, do you understand?"

Morgan looked so very sad and sorry that everybody decided to forgive him.

The children gave the puppy two biscuits,
and the dolls recovered their good spirits.
"Now that he has his own snack,
he won't want to chew on us,"
they smiled.

"What shall we do this afternoon?" asked the toys, after they'd had a tasty and peaceful lunch. It seemed that everyone had a different idea and Josephine wondered how to keep them pleased. "No arguing now," she cautioned. "I need a minute to think."

And she came up with a plan. "I'm going to cut little strips of paper and hold them all in my hand. Each of you will choose one, and the one who chooses the longest will get to decide what we're going to do this afternoon."

When each had chosen, they measured their papers. It seemed very clear that Dora's strip was the longest, though Quacky stuck two pieces together to make it seem as if he was the winner. "I want to go to the seaside," he said.

"You're in luck," replied Dora, who rightfully got to make the decision. "I want to go to the seaside, too!"

There was a great deal of excitement as they packed for the trip.

"How do you like this suit, Angelina?" Josephine asked, holding up the blue-and-white striped one.

"I'm sure it will be perfect," answered the curly-haired doll primly. She didn't really expect to go swimming. She was the type who only wanted to get her toes wet.

Dora demanded, "I want the green one!"

And Quacky paraded around in his trunks. "Don't you think pink is my color?" he asked Julia, while the Japanese dolls giggled.

When everybody, and their bathing suits, and their towels, and their buckets and shovels were packed and ready, Josephine loaded them onto the coach.

"Take us to the seashore!" she commanded.

The sand was pale gold and the sea a deep, soft blue. Josephine couldn't remember when she'd seen all the dolls and toys this happy. They hopped and jumped with joy, and laughed and danced around her by the shore.

She hitched a red string to Teddy's paw so that he could pull Quacky and two dolls on the donkey, for rides along the water's edge.

While, of course, the rest all wished to dig in the sand. It was just wet and firm enough, perfect for building and patting down. With the flashing of tiny spades and shovels in the sunlight, castles and moats, mountains and beach pies took shape.

"How about some bathing?" Josephine asked a little later. And they changed into their suits.

Very soon after, there was an unexpected splash as Angelina tumbled right into the sea.

Quacky flapped his wings from a nearby rock and called out "I'll help you! Don't be afraid!" He fluttered down to her side and helped the frightened little doll out of the water.

While she dried Angelina, Josephine looked at Quacky with a new kind of affection. "You were a hero and a gentleman just now," she said softly. "And I'm proud of you."

The rest of the afternoon passed like a sunny dream.

As the day wore on, Josephine called the toys together for a chat. "It's time to leave, but I have an errand to do on the way home. I want all of you to meet me back in the playroom in half an hour."

The dolls finished their wading and sun bathing and together with Josephine began their journey home. When their paths parted, they said, "We'll see you later, Josephine!"

She met John and Mama at the marketplace. Morgan was with them and followed very nicely. "Good boy," said Josephine, calling him gently. "Come with me."

They passed the stalls filled with flowers and fruit, vegetables and colorful packages. There were so many people and so many things to look at. "What can I buy as a present for the dolls?" she wondered. When they passed the candy counters Morgan barked with a delighted sound and Josephine had her answer. "A bag of chocolates, please," she asked.

Holding her parcel tightly, Josephine and the others headed home.

On the way back, she and John stopped to watch a circus parade coming into town.

There were scrambling monkeys and colorful clowns turning cartwheels. There were horses and bareback riders, but the most astonishing sight was a magnificent elephant, wearing a red tapestry blanket on his back. In front of him walked a mysterious man in a turban.

"We can make our own circus, can't we," whispered John to Josephine, as the exotic procession passed before them.

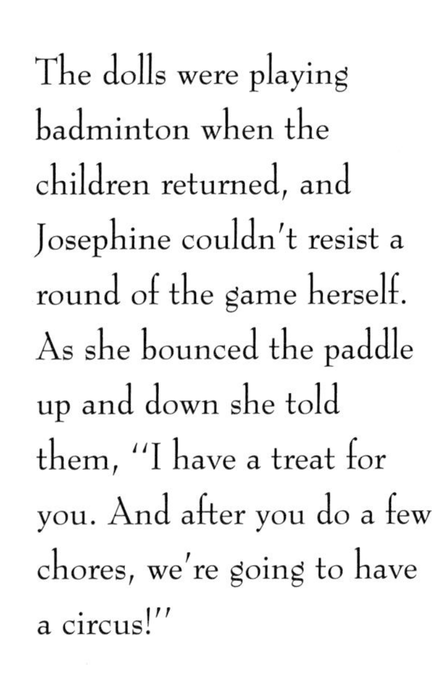

The dolls were playing badminton when the children returned, and Josephine couldn't resist a round of the game herself. As she bounced the paddle up and down she told them, "I have a treat for you. And after you do a few chores, we're going to have a circus!"

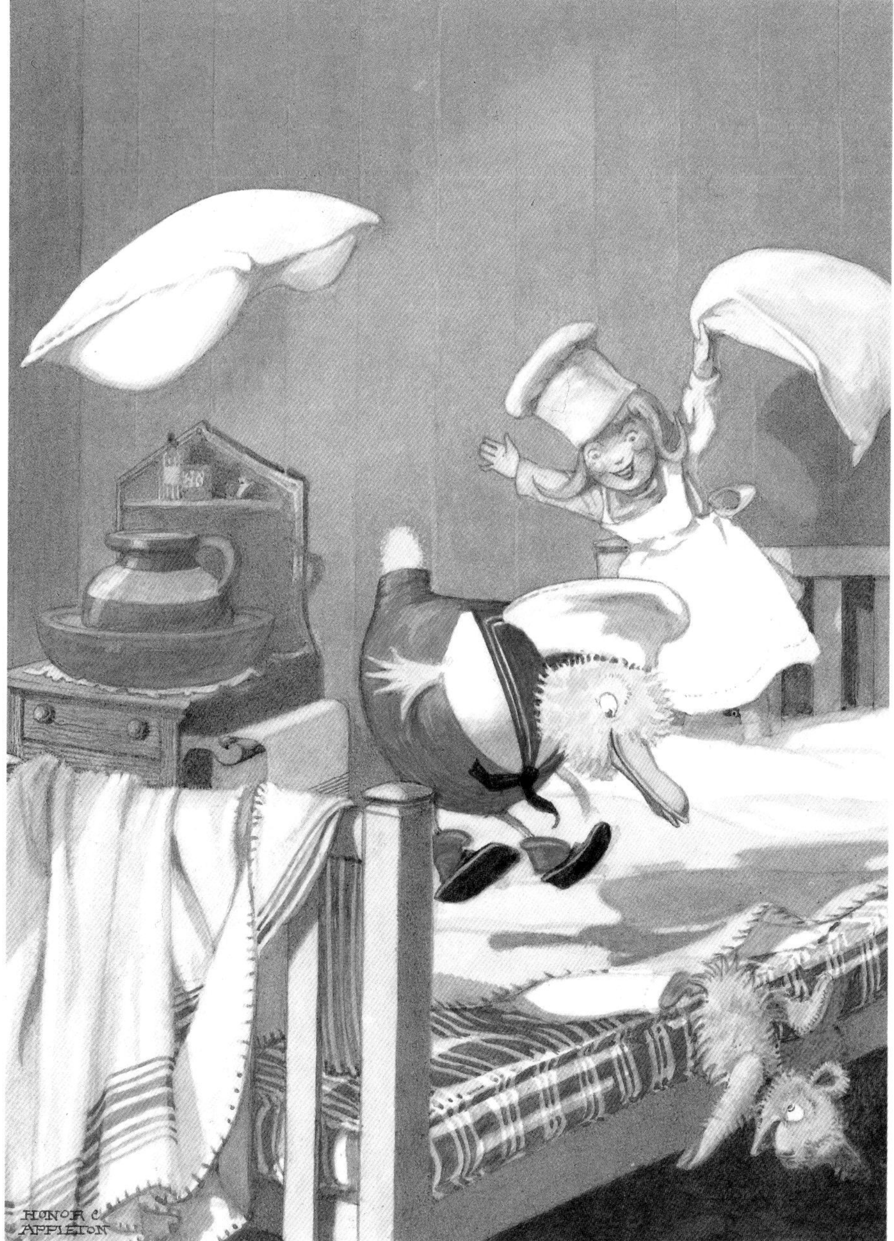


Quacky Jack, Dora, and Teddy had the job of making beds and plumping up pillows.

"Let's test these mattress springs," Quacky suggested. "I would like to know just how bouncy they can be!"

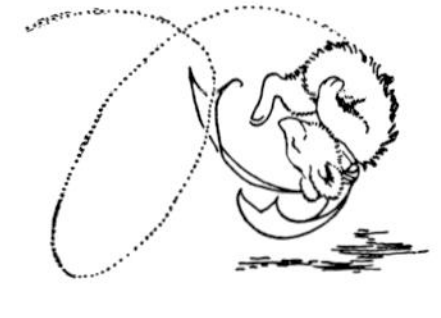

And they bounced
and bounced
and bounced
like rubber balls,
until Quacky bounced
and tumbled
and jumped
so high
that he flipped into the air
and landed across the room
feet first down on top of
the table where Josephine
had carefully laid out the
chocolates and candies
for a treat.

"My, what a pleasant surprise!" quacked Jack, catching his breath. And with his buckled black shoes he kicked a few of the sweets off of the table towards Granny and the Japanese dolls below.

"What am I going to do with you?" scolded Josephine, who couldn't help laughing at the same time. "Your manners are atrocious!"

To make up for his prank, he helped her give out candy to all the dolls. He was extremely polite, and charmed even Rosalie, in her flowered hat, who had been most shocked by his frisky behavior.

"Shall we have our circus now?" asked John.

Everyone yelled "Yes!" at once and immediately organized themselves into a parade.

The elephant carried Granny and the Postman doll while the rest frolicked about the playroom.

John tidied up the donkey so that he would look dapper and fancy.

Josephine made lots of tickets so that everyone would be able to attend. "Nobody will be left out," she said as she rummaged through the toy closet, determined to find every single creature, even the ones hiding shyly in corners. "Those who don't care to perform can be part of the audience; and *everyone* is important."

"Can I be the ringmaster?" asked Quacky Jack.

"Yes, you may!" the children answered.

And the performance began.

Clown threw Mr. Monkey up in the air six times and then performed a triple somersault himself.

Granny and the Japanese dolls danced a graceful dance and Quacky Jack did some clever magic tricks.

Julia astounded the audience by her amazing horseback act as she and her magnificent steed (who was really the modest donkey) galloped around the ring at a furious pace. When she balanced on only one foot, the audience clapped and clapped until their hands felt sore. Morgan barked with glee.

The last act was Teddy's. He lumbered into the center of the ring, bowed in a dignified way, and announced, "I've composed a poem for the occasion, and if you will permit me I shall recite it to you now."

This was his poem:

*I want to tell you how I feel;*
*To say just what I mean;*
*To say "I love you, all of you,*
*and, especially, Josephine."*

*She takes kind care of all of us;*
*she's gentle, fair, and fun.*
*She plays with us,*
*and laughs, and learns,*
*and when the day is done*
*we know that when*
*tomorrow comes*
*she'll be here. She's our friend.*
*That's why,*
*for children, dolls, and toys*
*good times can never end.*